To
fr

Nana July 14,
1975

The Cats from Summer Island

The Cats from Summer Island

by   EDITH UNNERSTAD

illustrated by Lilian Obligado

THE MACMILLAN COMPANY

New York   *1963*

Original title: *Kattorna Fran Sommaron*
© Raben & Sjogren, Stockholm, 1957
Barnangens Tryckerier AB,   Sthlm 1957

Translated from the Swedish by Holger Lundbergh
First Printing
Printed in the United States of America

It was the last night on Summer Island. Gretchen had cried herself to sleep with her cat, Rosamundus, in her arms. His soft fur was damp from her tears, for early the next morning the two would have to part.

Of course, Gretchen had known it all along. When she found the shy, spitting little kitten in the woods, her parents allowed her to keep him, but only for the summer. But Gretchen had thought that when fall came, Mother and Dad would love Rosamundus as much as she did. By then they would surely let him go back to the city with them.

1

Mother and Dad both admitted that Rosamundus was sweet now that he had become tame and well fed, and had stopped hissing and clawing. But they still didn't want to take him along.

Gretchen woke up as she felt Rosamundus wiggle from her arms. He jumped down and slipped quietly through the open door. But Gretchen didn't want him to leave, so she got up and padded out in the hall. On the stairway leading to the attic she thought she saw a pair of cat eyes sparkle in the dark, but then they disappeared. She heard a series of light thumps as the cat ran up the steps. Gretchen followed silently on tiptoe. She was afraid Rosamundus would sneak out the attic window.

But what was this? Bright, happy music was coming out of the attic door that stood ajar. Gretchen peeked in through the crack,

2

and was so surprised that she almost fell backward down the stairway.

Through the attic window, the moon shone full and bright. And in the moonlight all the cats on the island were dancing. Rufus, the red-haired cat from next door, was swinging around with the Landers' chubby little Suzy. Minette, Mrs. Owens' white kitten with the red bow, whirled backward with the Black Terror—the cat from the Pinecroft who spit at everybody. The Stevensons' twin cats, Ida and Frida, were dancing with each other, and Fisherman Seabell's old stiff-legged Moses was strutting about with Becky, the boarding-house cat. Rosamundus was in charge of the music. He sat at Gretchen's old toy piano and played a waltz. Tiger, the druggist's yellow-striped pussy, stood by the piano and blew on an old comb. And though the piano had lost two keys and the comb didn't have many

4

teeth left, the music didn't sound as bad as
you might expect.

"Now all together," Rosamundus meowed.

Not only could he play! He could speak,
as well!

5

And then all the cats sang:

"We're dancing and we're prancing here
  As the moonlight silver glows, meow, meow.
We're swinging and we're flinging here
  On light and nimble toes, meow, meow.

"Each pussy girl knows how to twirl
  When rousing music calls, meow, meow.
Each pussy boy can turn and whirl
  To Rosamundus' waltz, meow, meow."

They didn't sing particularly well. They meowed and whined and squealed. And old Moses hummed an off-key bass.

When the singing was over, Moses announced he had something to say. And the nine young cats sat down in a ring around him and pricked up their ears.

"We all know that the steamer *East Wind* is tied up at the pier," he said. "Tomorrow morning it leaves this island on its last trip for

6

the summer. Then all the people will go back to the city and desert you, you poor wretches. If that isn't unfair, I don't know what is."

"Meow, meow," all the cats chorused sadly. All except the Black Terror. "I think it'll be fine to get rid of them," he said. "Then at last I'll be able to sleep without somebody pulling my tail."

But Moses went on, "Only old Seabell stays here. And he can't afford to keep any cats except me. The rest of you will starve to death."

"Meow, how terrible," the cats wailed.

"Our people are not good to us," little Suzy sobbed.

"By the white hair in my black moustache," cried the Black Terror, "they're heartless."

"But the children are sweet," Rosamundus said. "They want us to come along to the city. Gretchen cried on me all night and now my fur is wringing wet."

"I won't miss my tail-puller and moustache-twitcher," said the Black Terror.

"My mistress already left last week," said Becky. "When she turned me out, she said: 'Good-by now, and take care of yourself and perhaps we'll meet next summer. In the meantime you'll have to live on mice.'"

"I'd like to see her try to live on mice when there are high snowdrifts on the island," sneered Moses. "Anyhow, there are hardly any mice left these days. The people all want a kitten in the summer, but then they leave the cat behind when they go. They say it's too hard for animals in the city, but I've heard there is plenty of milk and food and open doors to warm cellars the whole year around! And if you don't like the city, you can always move to the country. There are big houses there called barns that are full of cows you get sweet milk from."

8

"Think of being a barn cat," sighed Rufus.

"You know what my mistress said?" asked Minette. "She said that cats should never grow up, because then they get ugly, though they are cute when they are small."

"Isn't that the way with some people?" said the Black Terror, arching his back.

"Dear Grandpa Moses, what *are* we going to do?" asked Suzy.

"You must go out in the world and find new homes for yourselves," Moses replied. "But how will you get off the island? That's the question. Tomorrow all the people will go on board the steamer, so then it's too late."

9

"We can't very well swim to town, can we?" said Ida.

"Horrors, no," said Frida. "Water is so wet."

Gretchen could not keep quiet any longer. She flung open the door and rushed in. The cats were frightened and scampered off in all directions.

"I know," she cried. "You can all go on board the steamer tonight! I know Charlie, the deck boy. He can hide you and help you ashore in the city."

The cats quieted down when they saw it was only Gretchen standing there barefoot in her pajamas, right in the middle of a moonbeam. Rosamundus rubbed against her leg.

"Meow, meow," sounded hesitantly from the attic corners.

"Dear friends, speak to me," said Gretchen. "I know you can talk. I just heard you."

Then Moses came forward on his stiff legs

10

and said, "We don't want the people to know
that we can talk and understand what they
say. You must swear on what you like most
of all that you won't tell."

"I swear by Rosamundus never to tell that
cats can talk," promised Gretchen.

"Are you sure the deck boy won't tell on us?" the Black Terror asked anxiously. "Suppose he is one of those tail-pullers and moustache-twitchers who only wishes us bad luck?"

"Charlie!" exclaimed Gretchen. "Why, he lets me help tie up the boat!"

"I think he likes cats," said Moses. "Once when I lay on the dock sunning myself he offered me a fresh herring."

"Herring," moaned Becky. "I've only eaten a tough old field mouse and a few flies the whole week. Come on. Let's go see Charlie!"

"I'll follow you to the boat," said Moses.

"Come with us to town," Becky urged.

But Moses replied, "No, Seabell has been good to me ever since the day he pulled me out of the water and named me Moses. My summer people had tied me in a bag and thrown me into the sea when they went home.

Now Seabell is old and I have to lie at his feet at night to keep him warm. He could never go through a winter without me. Anyhow, I am too old for city life."

"Shouldn't we have one last dance before we go?" asked Minette.

"And we've got time for one last fight, too," said Rufus. "What do Tiger and the Black Terror say?"

"No, no," Gretchen pleaded. "Don't fight. It's so awful."

"Awful! We love to give each other a good drubbing," said Tiger. "Afterward we're just as good friends as before."

"But you'll wake up Mother and Dad," protested Gretchen.

"Gretchen is right," said Rosamundus. "Let's not fight tonight. But we must have one last dance."

So the boy cats asked the girl cats, and soon

they were all whirling in a gay waltz, their tails swinging behind them.

"Say, puss, that was really quite a match,
  Here are the marks where you gave me a scratch,
  If we fight all day, we'll dance all night,
  For that is a pussycat's greatest delight.
  Soon we'll dance the very last round,
  Soon we'll hear the warning sound
  Of the steamer's final toot,
  And at the break of day
  The ship will sail away."

Then they slipped silently down the stairs. Gretchen unlocked the front door, and they all hurried outside. They did not meet anyone on the road, which stretched out before them in the moonlight like a striped cat. Far away they heard a fox howl in the forest, and the little cats shivered, and hurried on. Soon they

14

came to the pier, and there lay the old excursion steamer, white and silent. Nobody stirred on board.

Gretchen tapped cautiously on one of the round portholes. Charlie, yawning widely, poked his head out, and smiled cheerfully

when he saw Gretchen with all of the cats.

"Sh!" warned Gretchen. "Can you smuggle the cats to town without anybody seeing them?"

Charlie said he could, so all the cats, except Moses, padded on board and hid under the bunk in his little cabin. Then Gretchen hurried home again, and Moses limped off to old Seabell's cottage.

When Gretchen was safely home in bed, rubbing her cold feet against each other to get them warm, she couldn't help laughing to herself and feeling a bit worried at the same time. What if Mother and Dad knew!

Early the next morning a crowd of people swarmed on the pier. All the summer visitors had to get back to the city with their children, for school was opening soon. When Gretchen arrived at the boat with her parents, she caught sight of Moses sitting on the dock with his

tail draped around his paws, gazing sadly at the steamer. Gretchen put her arms around him and whispered good-by.

"Say hello to all the cats for me," said Moses. "And tell them that if they only wash themselves clean and hold their tails in the air and don't let anybody sit on them, everything will turn out all right."

Gretchen hurried on board. Charlie was busy stowing bicycles and children's beds in the front of the boat. Gretchen had planned to take a look at the cats, but Mother pulled her along to the afterdeck. There sat Mr. Kurts from the Pinecroft with his son Albert, the Black Terror's tormentor. Mr. Kurts had his shotgun with him. "I planned to shoot the Black Terror before we left," he said. "But the cat must have suspected something, because he kept away." Gretchen grew pale when she heard this.

"Are you sick, little Cat Angel?" Albert teased her. "Surely not even you could like that horrible Black Terror." Gretchen's father wrinkled his forehead and said cats got to be mean if people were mean to them.

"Albert is such an animal-lover," said Mr. Kurts. "It was for his sake that we adopted that ugly cat."

"A tail-puller and moustache-twitcher is no animal-lover," muttered Gretchen.

"Listen to her," laughed Albert. "She can't stand a joke. You should at least be able to play with your pets."

"Boys will be boys, and that cat is a monster," said Mr. Kurts. "I hope the fox gets him in the winter."

"Now, now," said Mother. And it did seem as if neither she nor Dad approved of Mr. Kurts and Albert.

Suddenly the *East Wind* blew three long

20

blasts on its whistle. Just as they were beginning to pull in the gangplank and Charlie was casting off the rope, Mrs. Owens and her children came hurrying down the road at a gallop, and climbed on board at the last moment. As the steamer pulled out, Mrs. Owens panted, "It was the children's fault. They insisted on saying good-by to Minette, but we couldn't find her anywhere."

"We couldn't find Ida and Frida either," said the Stevenson girls, who were standing nearby.

"How very strange," said Gretchen's mother. "Our Rosamundus has also disappeared."

At that Gretchen could no longer suppress a laugh, so she ran down to Charlie's cabin. When the cats heard her voice, they came out from their hiding places.

Gretchen delivered the greeting from

Moses. She had to repeat it three times, so that Ida and Frida (who did not remember very well) could learn it all by heart—"Wash yourself clean, hold your tail in the air, and don't let anybody sit on you." And though they already had finished their morning baths, all the cats began to lick themselves again. Then they tried to hold their tails straight up, like exclamation points. And then they asked Gretchen to try to sit on them, so they could show her how quick they were.

Just then Charlie came in with a bottle of milk and some fat fried smelts. He had begged them from Miss Wave, the nice dining-room waitress. Each of the cats got one smelt apiece, and then they lapped up milk from Charlie's soap dish.

When Gretchen told Charlie what Mr. Kurts had said, the Black Terror pricked up his ears and stopped eating. He put one paw

22

on the half-finished smelt, so that nobody would snatch it.

Charlie became terribly angry. "Shoot this fine cat here! He looks just like my mother's cat Melvin, who died of old age last spring!" he cried. "Can't I take him home to Mother? We live in an old house in the south part of town, and there are plenty of rats in the cellar, so we need a strong cat. The Black Terror— what an awful name! Melvin the Second

sounds much better. Do you want to come and live with us, Melvin?"

Charlie reached out his hand, and the cat that used to hiss at everybody rubbed his head softly against the boy's leg. Then he picked up the half-eaten smelt and laid it in the boy's hand.

"I suppose he means that I should eat it," Charlie said. "Well, why not? Cats are clean animals, and the smelt is well fried, so there's no harm in it." When Charlie had eaten it, he said, "Thank you, Melvin. Now you and I are friends for life, since we have eaten from the same smelt."

After Charlie had left, the cat sighed contentedly. "By the white hair in my black moustache, for a human being he isn't so bad."

At Klack Island, where the *East Wind* made a brief stop, a big dog came on board with his master. It quickly picked up the trail of the

24

cats, and the thud of his big paws could be heard all through the boat. Abruptly he stopped outside the door to Charlie's cabin, and growled and barked till the door shook as he tried to get in.

Eight of the cats flew like lightning up onto the shelf under the ceiling. Only one stayed on the floor, with his back arched and his tail as bushy as a little Christmas tree. When the dog finally managed to make the latch give way and the door flew open, the cat was ready to meet him. First he gave the dog a good cuffing. Then he jumped on his neck and hung on with all his claws. Howling with terror,

the dog set off and raced down the hall with the cat on his back.

The deck stewardess was standing in the hall, powdering her nose. The next minute she was sprawled on the floor. Looking up, she only caught a glimpse of something striped disappearing around the corner.

"Tiger!" Gretchen called anxiously from the door. "Come back here, Tiger!"

"A *tiger!* HELP!" screamed the stewardess.

Everyone came running. There were the chief officer, the fireman, Miss Wave, and some passengers.

"Where is he? Did he bite you?—Nonsense, there's no tiger here. It must have been that dog that got on board at Klack Island," they said.

"I know what tigers look like," the stewardess cried. "It was black-and-yellow striped. And terribly big!"

26

"Could it possibly have been him?" asked the chief officer, pointing at Tiger, who had ridden the dog all around the boat at a terrible pace and now had jumped off his back and came sneaking along the hall.

"That one?" the stewardess repeated, bewildered.

"Well, it has yellow stripes, all right," said Miss Wave. "So that was the big terrible tiger!"

Then everybody laughed and teased the stewardess until she finally believed it actually was the little cat who had knocked her over.

Miss Wave, the waitress, took Tiger to her little cabin and fed him lobster and sardines and salmon fins. Tiger ate till his stomach was like a ball. And Miss Wave stroked him and told him what a brave cat he was and how he had scared the boat's most ill-tempered stewardess.

Gretchen, who had followed them, heard

all this. "Excuse me," she said. "Wouldn't you like to have Tiger for your own cat, Miss Wave? He needs a home."

"But I don't have a home," Miss Wave explained. "I live on board. And next week I start work on a ship that goes to Africa."

"Oh, Tiger would certainly love to go to Africa—would you like to be a ship's cat, Tiger?"

"Meow," Tiger replied.

"I declare," said Miss Wave. "It sounded exactly as if he answered yes."

"That's just what he did," said Gretchen.

"Tell me, Tiger, you like Miss Wave, don't you?"

"Meow, meow, meow!" said Tiger, and looked lovingly at Miss Wave, with his head to one side.

"What a clever little darling!" Miss Wave exclaimed, delighted. "I'll take him. He can come with me to Africa."

Then she gave Gretchen five dimes—one dime for each paw and one for the tail. And then Gretchen shook hands with Miss Wave and kissed Tiger good-by on the ear.

Then she went up to the dining room and had beefsteak and fried onions with Mother and Dad. Far away on the afterdeck lay the dog, huddled under a bench. He looked very embarrassed, as if he would never go cat-hunting again.

The *East Wind* stopped at one island after the other, collecting parents and children and

29

furniture. At last it steamed in toward the pier in the big city. Gretchen made a final quick visit to the cats. She held Rosamundus up to the porthole and said, "Do you see the trees there behind the National Museum? That's the Museum Park. Get over there as fast as you can when you get ashore, and we'll meet there. I live nearby, and I'll try to get a home for you in our apartment house. Then we can meet every day." Then she kissed all the cats on the ear and hurried ashore with her parents.

Only after all the passengers had left and all the freight was unloaded did Charlie find time to help his guests.

The Black Terror and Tiger remained on board, of course. But when the pier seemed quite empty for a moment and neither the captain nor the crew were looking in that direction, Charlie let the other seven cats

ashore. With their tails straight up, the cats marched with great dignity across the gangplank.

Some cars were parked on the dock. The cats had never seen an automobile before. On Summer Island there weren't any cars—only Seabell's wheelbarrow, a handcart from the boardinghouse, and the bicycles and baby buggies that belonged to the summer people.

"Look!" cried Becky. "The motorboats move on land here."

"Those aren't motorboats. They're some

sort of animal. Can't you see they have eyes?" meowed Minette.

"Animals don't have windows all around, do they?" asked Rosamundus.

"They're houses," said Rufus. "You could probably live in them, though they are small."

"Perhaps they're our new homes," Suzy wondered.

"Then I want to live in that pretty one with the curtains," said Ida.

"Me, too," said Frida.

The one with the curtains was a big blue car. The door stood open, and Rufus peeked inside and saw that there were lovely sofas to lie on. He jumped on the back seat. Ida and Frida were about to do the same, when the owner appeared from behind the car. He got in and sat down at the wheel and slammed the door shut. And in a jiffy he had driven off with Rufus.

32

"The house m-m-moves!" Ida stuttered.

"It was a m-m-motorboat after all," stammered Frida.

Then another car came right at them and Ida and Frida were so scared that they rushed straight across the street and right into the main lobby of the Grand Hotel. Dizzy with fright, they raced through halls and lobbies and dining rooms and upstairs and downstairs and got all tangled up in the feet of the guests and servants and waiters and created a terrible uproar. At last they landed in the big kitchen.

They never got any farther, because the chefs and scullery boys thought they were so sweet that they wanted to keep them.

And everyone knows how well off hotel cats are. So Ida and Frida settled down in the

Grand Hotel and grew fat and splendid and never longed for Summer Island again.

Rufus had slipped down from the seat when the car started off. He lay there quivering and couldn't understand at all what he had got himself into. The car drove all through the city and many miles out in the country and didn't stop until it came to a big farm. There the owner got out and a little red-haired boy with friendly blue eyes came running.

"Oh, Dad, you've bought a cat for me!" he cried, as Rufus crawled out. The father stared in surprise at the cat, which he had not noticed during the entire trip. But he kept a straight face, for he suddenly remembered that it was his son's birthday, and he had forgotten to buy him a present.

"That's right," he said. "I picked this one because he has the same color of hair as you and me."

Then Rufus saw that the little boy and his father had red hair. And he thought: "Perhaps I'm going to like it here." And a little later when he saw the barn with all the cows, he was quite sure that he would. For he loved milk more than anything else.

Suzy and Becky had also become frightened when the car came straight at them, and they hid behind a pile of empty herring crates. There they sat, peeking out at automobiles, and buses, and streetcars, thinking what a fantastic racket they made. Then Suzy said they must hurry to the Museum Park and look for Gretchen. But Becky said she wanted to find a home by herself, so the two separated and went their own ways.

Becky hurried along the street. She looked at the gulls that circled over the harbor, snatching a fish now and then from the water.

Her stomach shrieked with hunger, for it was a long time since she had eaten that smelt on the steamer.

Then she came to a bridge. She did not dare get into the traffic there. Instead she jumped up on the broad stone railing, and began to walk across. But then she happened to look down at the water. There sat a smelt fisherman in his boat, cranking up his big round net. Only three little smelts danced and glistened in the bottom of the net. Becky licked her mouth. She stretched far out and looked hungrily at the little smelts below. The fisherman lowered his net again with an unhappy shake of his head. And then suddenly—bang!—the cat lost her balance and fell with a splash into the water. This time when the fisherman cranked up his net, it was full of smelts. And right in the middle of the smelts wriggled Becky!

38

"You're a queer fish," said the man. "But you bring good luck. I've never caught so many smelts at one time before. So help yourself and eat!"

He emptied the net in the boat. Becky was wet and cold. But she forgot that as she ravenously attacked the fish and began to eat. She ate and ate while the fisherman continued to lower and raise his net and fill the boat with fish. Then she purred so nicely, thanking him for the wonderful meal, that the fisherman was quite touched.

It took him three trips to carry the smelts to the fish market because he only had one basket. And while he was away, Becky sat in the boat and kept watch on the haul.

When all the fish had been delivered, the fisherman took his new friend under his arm and went home to his little house. That night Becky slept on a folded old burlap bag near

40

the tile stove. Every morning after that they went to the boat together, for the fisherman thought that Becky brought him good luck. And if they didn't get any smelts, they shared the fisherman's sandwich. And every night Becky slept in the corner by the tile stove, and purred lovely good-night songs for the fisherman. Being a fishing cat, she thought, was much better than being a boardinghouse cat.

And how did Suzy make out? Well, she mistook the Navy Yard Island for the Museum Park, since both had a lot of green trees. She looked for Gretchen and Rosamundus all over the island but couldn't find them. Then she went out across a bridge onto another little island. On the farthest point, in front of a cozy yellow house, sat an old retired navy captain and his little round wife, drinking coffee in the sunshine. When they caught sight of Suzy they called to her and gave her some cream to drink.

"What a sweet little pussy," said the old lady. "It looks like a gray ball of yarn. And its little tongue is pink as a rose petal. Wouldn't it be nice with a cat here, Peter! Why don't we keep this one, if nobody claims it?"

"Oh, the owner will surely show up," said the captain. "No one would part with such a fine cat."

42

But who would come looking for Suzy? She stayed with the old couple, and soon she followed the captain on his daily walks and went marketing with the little round wife. And in the evenings she lay in their laps as they sat rocking before the fire. She was just like a child to them. Suzy had found a real home for herself.

When Gretchen arrived home she went

looking for a home for Rosamundus. She went downstairs to ask the janitor's wife if she wanted a nice cat. But when the janitor's wife heard it was gray, she said no. The only kind of cat she wanted was a white one, because that's the kind she had had when she was a girl. She had called her Snow White, and she had never forgotten her.

Then Gretchen called on all the neighbors in the building, but nobody wanted a cat. She hung her head sadly as she walked to the Museum Park to give the bad news to Rosamundus.

"Meow, meow," she heard from someplace high up in the air. There sat Rosamundus and Minette in a tree. They clambered down backward, the way cats do.

"Forgive me for tagging along after Rosamundus," said Minette, "but I didn't know where to turn in this dangerous city."

Gretchen stared at her. "Minette! I forgot! You are all white!" she exclaimed. "You don't even have one dark hair."

"Should I?" asked Minette anxiously.

"Of course not," said Gretchen. And then she told her what the janitor's wife had said.

"Oh, let's go there!" Minette urged.

But Gretchen was crying into Rosamundus' soft gray fur.

"I won't stay with Dad and Mother any longer, if they won't let me keep you here,"

she said. "If you are going out in the world to find a new home, I want to go with you."

"First you must take me to the janitor's wife," insisted Minette.

"And we need to take some food along, if we are going out in the big wide world," said Rosamundus.

So Gretchen went home, and the two cats followed her. Rosamundus waited on the stairs

while she carried Minette in to the janitor's wife.

"What did she say?" asked Rosamundus, when Gretchen came out.

"She didn't believe it was true," Gretchen told him. "She said, 'Snow White! How wonderful! Come have some meat-loaf, my lovely little cat!'"

Then Gretchen went up to her apartment to make some sandwiches and get some change from her piggy bank. But as she stood in the pantry buttering the bread, she overheard Dad and Mother talking in the living room.

"We've made a very foolish mistake," said Dad. "I'd better go over to the island next Sunday on the fishing tug and bring Rosamundus back. I can't understand how we could have left the poor creature behind. If he doesn't starve to death, the fox will surely get him, poor thing."

"And if we have a cold winter, he may freeze to death."

"And even if he does survive, he'll get wild and turn into a hunter. Then someone like Mr. Kurts will come along in the spring and shoot him."

"There's no doubt about it," said Mother. "We should have brought him with us."

"But didn't you feel that a cat would be a lot of trouble in the city?" asked Dad.

"Oh, we'll soon get used to it," said Mother.

"Well, then, it's agreed that I'll go get Rosamundus. Won't Gretchen be surprised!" said Dad.

Gretchen stood very still in the pantry. She felt so happy that she pressed the buttered bread against herself, and her red jacket got a big grease spot on it. Her first thought was to run in and hug Dad and Mother and cry, "Hurrah!" But instead she flew out of the kitchen and down the stairs. She picked up her cat and raced up again and into the living room with him.

"Here I am with our beloved Rosamundus," she sang out, and put him down right in the middle of the table.

"Well, I declare!" exclaimed Dad and Mother in unison.

And Rosamundus stood there with his tail high in the air and looked from one to the other. Then he calmly sat down and began to wash himself.